THE
HOME RUN
KINGS

BABE RUTH • • • HENRY AARON

by Clare and Frank Gault

SCHOLASTIC INC.
New York Toronto London Auckland Sydney

Photo Credits

All photographs from United Press International except: Culver Pictures: 29; New York Public Library Picture Collection; 32; Wide World Photos: 62, 64.

ISBN 0-590-45530-3

Copyright © 1974 by Clare S. Gault and Frank M. Gault.
All rights reserved. Published by Scholastic Inc.

12 11 10 9 8 7 6 5 4 3 2 1   5   2 3 4 5 6 7/9

Printed in the U.S.A.

THE
HOME RUN
KINGS

BABE RUTH • • • HENRY AARON

A note from the authors

Many ballplayers hit home runs from time to time. Some players may even hit a lot of home runs in a single year. But very few players are able to hit lots of home runs year after year.

When you think about home-run hitters, there are probably several players you remember. But there are two special players you will always remember — Henry Aaron and Babe Ruth. They are the greatest home-run hitters of all time — the home run kings.

Babe Ruth lived and played many years ago. He held the home-run record for a long time. Henry Aaron is still playing and hitting home runs. He has hit more than Babe Ruth. And every time he hits another home run, he sets a new record.

It will probably be many, many years before any other player comes even close to Henry Aaron's home-run record. And perhaps no one ever will.

Clare and Frank Gault

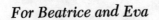
For Beatrice and Eva

George Herman "Babe" Ruth

George stood in front of the tall iron gate and watched the gatekeeper unlock the bolt. The gatekeeper slid the bolt back with a clang and swung the gate open.

George gulped hard. He was trying his best to look unafraid, but down deep in his stomach he was very nervous. It was late in the afternoon and the whole place looked gloomy. The buildings behind the gate were made of dull red brick. There was a large yard to one side. And the entire place was surrounded by a high fence. A sign on the front of the main building said "St. Mary's Industrial School."

This was to be his new home and new school. He knew that he would be sleeping, eating, and going to classes here. He wouldn't be seeing his mother and father or any of his friends for a long, long time. It was all very strange to him. He had never been to a place like this and he didn't know anyone here.

George really didn't know why he was being sent away from home. How could he understand? He was only seven years old. He knew that he had caused his father and mother a lot of trouble. Was this why they were sending him away?

George's father and mother ran a saloon near the Baltimore, Maryland, waterfront. Tough longshoremen who loaded and unloaded the ships that docked nearby came to the saloon to stand at the bar and drink. So did seamen just off their boats after months at sea.

George's father and mother had to

spend long hours at the saloon every day and night. George spent most of his time in the streets or down at the docks or in the saloon. The year was 1902 and the Baltimore waterfront was a rough place.

George knew that his father and mother worried about him. They got upset with him too — for example, when he took money from the cash box at the saloon or from his mother's purse.

People laughed and thought it was a joke when George drank whiskey customers gave him at the saloon, but his parents were angry. And they didn't like it when he chewed tobacco. George didn't especially like to chew tobacco either, but he saw that nearly everyone else around the waterfront did, so he figured it was the thing to do.

George's father and mother took him to the neighborhood school several times, but George didn't like school. Most of the time, there was no one home to make him go, so he just went out into the streets to play instead.

Now George was being sent to live and go to school at St. Mary's. It was in Baltimore, but far from the waterfront. George didn't like the looks of the place. He didn't want to go there, but he had no choice.

St. Mary's was run by the Xaverian Brothers, a Catholic order of priests. One of the Brothers checked George into the school, gave him a bed and locker in a large room with a number of other boys, and told him that he would have to live by the rules.

George wasn't exactly sure what "living by the rules" meant. But he felt sure he wouldn't like it.

George had no trouble meeting and getting to know the other boys though. A couple of the larger boys tried to test him just a bit, to see if he was tough. But George let them know right away that he was ready and able to fight anyone, so they figured he was OK and let him be.

Most of the boys at St. Mary's were like his friends down at the waterfront. Some were orphans. Others had run away from home and had been picked up from the Baltimore streets. Nearly all of them were tough and from families with no money. They had been sent to St. Mary's in hopes the Brothers could give them an education and teach them a trade.

The next morning, very early, George and the other boys were awakened by one of the Brothers. He had them march to breakfast and then to class. None of the other boys seemed to think this unusual, but George did. He wasn't used to waking up so early and being marched around.

Classes that morning seemed to last a long, long time. George felt like he was in a cage. But he knew that he couldn't run away or get over the high fence, so he had to put up with it.

Finally, recess came and all the boys rushed into the school yard. Everyone started running and shouting. And it didn't take long for a fight to start. One boy ran into another and, in a flash, they were on the ground wrestling. All the boys gathered in a circle around them to cheer. George pressed in too. He liked a good fight.

The cheering and yelling grew louder and louder. Then suddenly it stopped. The yard became very quiet. The boys on the ground stopped fighting. George looked around. There stood a huge man, one of the Brothers. He was dressed in a Brother's robe with a rope sash tied around his waist. To George, he looked like a giant.

"Brother Matthias," whispered one of the boys.

Brother Matthias just stood and looked around the yard for a minute or two, then walked away. The two boys who were fighting got up, dusted themselves off, and went back to playing. So did all the others.

"Wow," said George to one of the other boys, "everybody is sure scared of him. What does he do, beat you?"

The other boy laughed. "Brother Matthias? Heck no, he's a real nice guy."

Later that day, George met Brother Matthias. He walked up to George after supper and said, "We're glad to have you with us, George." He smiled and shook George's hand.

George mumbled something in reply and felt shy. But he liked Brother Matthias right away. Brother Matthias was a big man — well over six feet tall. He looked strict, but friendly, and all the boys seemed to like him. Brother Matthias taught classes at St. Mary's. He also coached the school's baseball teams. When spring came, he asked George to play baseball.

Baseball was new to George, and he liked the game at once. The position he liked to play best was catcher. He had a problem though. George was left-handed and the school had no catcher's mitt for a left-handed catcher. This meant he had to wear the mitt on his left hand while catching the ball, then flip it off fast in order to throw with his left hand back to the pitcher or to a base.

George practiced hard and became such a good catcher that Brother Matthias put him on a team with boys three and four years older than he was.

Then one day, when George was about 14 years old, something happened that changed his baseball career. George's team was playing another team. Things were going badly. The starting pitcher was hit hard and gave up five runs in the first inning. A second pitcher was brought in, but he couldn't do much better. Then a third pitcher was tried. And he was hit hard too. By this time, the game was completely one-sided. And George began to laugh and make fun of his own pitcher.

Suddenly, Brother Matthias stopped the game and walked out onto the field. He drew George aside.

"What are you laughing at?" Brother Matthias asked George.

George was still laughing. "Our pitchers are getting their brains knocked out, and it just struck me funny."

Brother Matthias looked at George for a minute. "All right, George, you pitch."

George stopped laughing. "I never pitched in my life," he said. "I can't pitch."

"Oh, but you must know a lot about it," Brother Matthias said. "You know enough to know that your friends are having trouble. Go ahead and show us how it's done." Brother Matthias wanted to teach George a lesson.

George was taken by surprise. He didn't even know how to stand on the pitcher's mound. But he had to try.

George wound up and threw his first pitch. It was a strike, a good fast ball. George was surprised. He felt strangely at home and comfortable on the mound. He threw another pitch. It was a strike too. Then he tried a curve ball. It completely fooled the batter who swung and missed. Strike three.

Before very long, the side was out. And George went the rest of the game without allowing any more runs. George was excited. It was fun to pitch, even more fun than catching. Brother Matthias was happy too. He had found another pitcher.

George worked hard on his pitching. Often Brother Matthias put in extra time practicing with him. Soon George became the best pitcher in the area. His curve ball was especially good, but it didn't always fool the batters.

"You have a bad habit," Brother Matthias told him. "Every time you get ready to throw your curve ball, you stick your tongue out of the corner of your mouth. When the batter sees that, he knows what to expect and it's much harder to fool him."

George had to think very hard not to stick his tongue out when he was about to throw a curve ball. Every time he forgot, his tongue would pop out. It was a tough habit to break. In fact, he never did break it until he was in the major leagues. But he tried.

George had to work hard in school too. Because he liked and respected Brother Matthias so much, he tried his best. All the boys had to learn a trade so they could earn a living when they were out of school. George learned tailoring and shirtmaking.

George lived and went to school at St. Mary's for many years. Finally, it was almost time to leave. He was 19 years old and almost as tall as Brother Matthias. He knew his trade and was ready.

Then one day, as he was practicing in the school yard, Brother Matthias walked up with a stranger. "George," Brother Matthias said, "this is Mr. Dunn, Manager of the Baltimore Orioles baseball team. He'd like to talk to you."

Mr. Dunn said, "George, Brother Matthias tells me that you can pitch. How would you like to play professional baseball?"

George was so surprised he couldn't speak.

Mr. Dunn went on. "Now, about your salary . . . "

George gasped. "You mean you'd pay me?"

"Sure, George," Mr. Dunn continued. "I'll start you out at six hundred a year."

"You mean six hundred — dollars?" George croaked.

"That's right." Mr. Dunn laughed. "And we'll pay you even more if you're as good as the Brothers here say you are."

The Brothers at St. Mary's had been asked to be on the lookout for good baseball players and Brother Matthias had put in George's name. George was flabbergasted. A professional baseball team was offering him money to do what he liked best. And it sounded like a lot more fun than tailoring or making shirts.

The day George was to leave, he had plenty of doubts though. He was excited about playing professional baseball. But he was nervous about leaving St. Mary's. This had been his home, almost the only one he had ever known. And he was afraid he might fail. He wanted Brother Matthias to be proud of him.

George said good-bye to St. Mary's and to his friends. Brother Matthias shook his hand warmly. "You'll make it, George," he said.

Spring training camp for the Orioles was held in Fayetteville, North Carolina. George was the youngest rookie there. He was big, but still a bit awkward, and he had a round face like a baby's. When the older players saw George they started calling him "Babe."

Everything in the world outside St. Mary's gate and high fence was new and wonderful to George. His first big surprise came when he found out that the Orioles team paid for his hotel room and meals. The team ate in the hotel dining room. They ordered from a big menu and were served by the hotel waiters. George had been used to the plain and simple meals at St. Mary's. Now, he discovered that he could order what he liked and as much as he liked.

For breakfast, George had two orders of eggs with bacon, three large orders of pancakes and syrup, a stack of french toast, and coffee. At last, he stopped eating and pushed himself back from the table. He sighed a big sigh. Then he noticed that half the team had been watching him eat.

"I wouldn't have believed it if I hadn't seen it with my own eyes," said Roger Pippen, one of the Orioles.

"Is he human?" catcher Ben Egan asked.

George grinned. "A guy's got to be strong to play ball," he said.

George continued to amaze his teammates through lunch and dinner. Steaks, roast beef, pork chops, chicken, ham, turkey, and plenty of mashed potatoes helped down by bread and rolls.

In the morning, George was so excited about being out in the world, he got up at five o'clock just to walk around the center of town and look into store windows. Then he went to the railroad station to watch the trains pull in and out. But he got back to the hotel in time to be first in line for breakfast.

George was crazy about the hotel's elevator. He made excuses to ride it up and down. One day, he talked the regular elevator operator into letting him run it. It was an old elevator with an open cab and George almost killed himself when he stuck his head out between floors while the elevator was still moving.

The other Oriole players thought it was fun to tease George. And George didn't mind. He rather liked the attention. Soon everyone was calling him "Babe." He was hardly ever called "George" anymore.

In training, Babe worked hard on his pitching with Ben Egan, the catcher, but he always took his full turn at batting practice too. Babe liked to hit, and he felt that a pitcher should get his share of hits. He didn't want to be an easy out in the line-up.

Near the end of spring training, Babe got his first paycheck. He took it and ran out to buy a new bicycle. For his whole life he had wanted one. Now, for the first time, he could afford to buy one.

Babe's bicycle gave the other Oriole

players something else to laugh at. Most of them had cars and thought it silly that a big fellow like Babe wanted to ride a bicycle. But Babe didn't care. He loved his new bike. And instead of walking around town early in the morning, he rode his bicycle.

When the season opened, Babe got a chance to pitch right away and started winning. But before the season had gone very far, he was traded to the Boston Red Sox. The Baltimore club needed money and were selling some of their players to other clubs.

Boston sent Babe to their minor-league farm team in Providence, Rhode Island. Babe helped them win the pennant there, but returned to Boston in time to pitch in four games, winning two and losing one.

The next season, 1915, things looked great for the Boston Red Sox and for Babe.

Lots of boys played baseball at St. Mary's. George Ruth was a catcher in the Senior League at this time.

This is the ball field at St. Mary's where George first played baseball. Inset picture shows George with his catcher's mitt and mask.

Babe Ruth was a regular on the Boston Red Sox pitching staff in 1915. They won the World Series. Left to right: George Foster, Carl Mays, Ernie Shore, Babe Ruth, and Dutch Leonard.

As a pitcher for the Boston Red Sox, Babe won 87 games plus the three games he pitched in World Series play.

In his first year with the New York Yankees, Babe played the outfield and hit 54 home runs.

Babe and Lou Gehrig were a great home-run-hitting pair. They were Yankee teammates for many years.

After he retired as an active player, Babe was a coach for one season with the Brooklyn Dodgers.

Babe was always popular with young fans. Even after
he retired from playing, he always drew a crowd.

This time Babe stayed with the Boston club for the whole season. He won 18 games while losing only six, the best won-lost percentage in the major leagues. At the plate, Babe batted .315, a very high batting average for a pitcher. He hit four home runs. One of them went clear over the roof at the Polo Grounds in New York. It was only the second time that had ever been done.

Babe was earning a reputation at bat, as well as on the pitching mound.

In 1916, Babe continued to pitch well. He won 23 games while losing 12. That tied him with another pitcher for the most wins, but Babe had a 1.75 earned run average and that was tops. At bat, he slipped to a .272 average.

The Red Sox won the American League pennant and played the World Series against the Brooklyn Dodgers. Babe pitched the second game. He gave up a run in the first inning, but blanked the Dodgers for the next 13 innings and won it 2 to 1 in 14 innings. The Red Sox won the series in five games, and Babe didn't get another chance to pitch.

The next year, Babe again won 23 games while losing 13. At bat, he hit .325. The Red Sox failed to win the pennant, however.

The Red Sox teams of those years had a number of fine pitchers and were great at fielding. But they were weak in hitting and producing runs. At the beginning of the 1918 season, the manager made an unusual suggestion to Babe. "You're big and strong, Babe, why don't you play the outfield on the days you're not pitching?" He wanted Babe's batting power in the line-up every day.

Babe said he would be happy to try, and in the following season he played nearly every game. Because of World War I, fewer games were played that year. Babe won 13 games pitching, batted .300, and hit 11 home runs.

The Red Sox won the pennant again and faced the Chicago Cubs in the World Series. Babe pitched the opening game and won it 1 to 0. He pitched again in the fourth game and won that, 3 to 2. He held the Cubs scoreless for the first seven innings. The Red Sox won the series four games to two.

Babe pitched in a total of three World Series games, one in 1916 and two in 1918. He won all three games and pitched 29 innings of shutout baseball in a row in World Series play. That was a new pitching record.

The next season, Babe continued pitching and playing the outfield so that he could be in the line-up every day. But part of the way through the season, he began to feel the strain would be too much, and said so to his manager. "Well," asked the manager, "which would you rather do, hit or pitch?"

"I certainly like to hit . . ." began Babe. It was as far as he got.

"Fine, fine," cut in the manager, "we'll keep you in the outfield then."

Babe still managed to win eight games while losing five games pitching that year. He hit .322 though, and set a new record in home runs, 29. From that time on, Babe was known as an outfielder and a hitter. His job wasn't pitching anymore, although he did pitch five more games over the next 13 years just to show people that he could still hurl the baseball. He won all five of those games.

The next year, 1920, the New York

Yankees made a huge trade and money deal with Boston and got Babe for their team. Up until that time, the Yankees had never won a pennant, but they were building a new team and Babe was an important part of their plan.

Babe helped the Yankees win their first pennant in 1921 and six more pennants after that. In the 15 years Babe was a Yankee, they won seven pennants and four World Series. Eleven of those years, Babe hit 40 or more home runs and for four of those years, he hit 50 or more home runs.

Whenever Babe decided to swing, he took a full cut at the ball. When he connected, the ball went. One day, he hit a line drive that went between the pitcher's legs and traveled over the center fielder's head for a triple.

One time, Babe really hit the ball, but he got under it too much. It went nearly straight up, far up. While Babe ran around first base and then to second, the second baseman circled and circled and circled under the ball. When it finally came down, the second baseman was so dizzy he missed it. Babe was safe on second base, but when he saw the box score it had been ruled an error, not a hit. Babe was mad. When he saw the official scorer, he asked, "What does a ballplayer have to do in this league to get a hit?"

"Hit the ball out of the infield," answered the scorer. That shut Babe up.

Babe hit lots of balls out of the infield and all the way out of the ball park. He hit a total of 714 home runs during regular season play. It is estimated that he hit another 300 or so in exhibition games. He became famous for being able to predict when he'd hit a home run. He could even predict where he'd hit it.

Once during a tight game, Babe hit a ball down the right field line and into the bleacher seats. He was half way around the bases when he heard the umpire shout, "Foul ball."

Babe returned to home plate and glared at the umpire. "It was foul, just by inches," explained the umpire.

"OK," said Babe, "I'll make this one fair." And he did. He hit the next pitch in almost the same place, only it was fair by inches.

Another time, the Yankees were all tied up in an extra-inning ball game. It was getting later and later. Babe noticed that the team's traveling secretary was getting more and more nervous. "What's the matter?" Babe asked.

"We have reservations on the train right after the ball game, and it doesn't look like we'll be there on time," answered the secretary.

"Why didn't you say so?" Babe said.

Five minutes later, Babe went to the plate and hit a home run that won the ball game. And the team got to the train on time.

In 1932, the Yankees met the Chicago Cubs in the World Series. There was bad feeling between the two clubs. The Yankees won the first two games in New York and the Series moved to Chicago. In the third game, the Chicago fans started calling Babe names. Some fans even threw rotten tomatoes at him as he played his position in left field.

In the middle of that game, Babe came to bat with men on base. The crowd booed. "I'll show them," Babe thought to himself. As he came to the plate, he pointed to the bleacher seats in center field. The crowd laughed and razzed him.

The pitcher threw a blazing fast ball and Babe watched it go by. Even before the umpire could call the pitch, Babe raised his right arm and shouted "strike one" on himself.

The pitcher threw again, and again it was a fast ball right down the middle. "Strike two," shouted Babe raising his right arm. Babe pointed to the center field bleachers again while the crowd jeered.

The next pitch came in. Babe swung with all his might and connected. The ball went far out into center field and landed up in the bleacher seats, right where Babe had pointed. It was a home run. Babe danced around the bases while the Cubs and their fans were stunned.

Thanks to Babe's home run, the Yankees won that third game. They went on to win the fourth also, taking the Series in four straight games.

As a baseball hero and home-run hitter,

Babe always attracted lots of kids. They liked to get his autograph and to talk to him. And Babe liked kids. He felt comfortable with them. Often, he would visit hospitals and orphanages to see if he could cheer them up. And of course, he went back to see Brother Matthias and the boys at St. Mary's as often as he could.

After all, he was one of the boys from St. Mary's and he always would be. St. Mary's was home to him. It was where he first threw and hit a baseball. And it was where he got his start toward becoming one of the home run kings.

Babe Ruth's major league record — as a pitcher

Year	Games pitched	Innings pitched	Won	Lost	Per-centage	Hits given up	Runs allowed	Bases on balls	Strike outs	Earned run average
1914	4	22	2	1	.667	21	12	7	2	3.91
1915	32	218	18	6	.750	166	80	85	112	2.44
1916	44	324	23	12	.657	230	83	118	170	1.75
1917	41	326	23	13	.639	244	93	108	128	2.02
1918	20	166	13	7	.650	125	51	49	40	2.22
1919	17	133	8	5	.615	148	59	58	30	2.97
1920	1	4	1	0	1.000	3	4	2	0	4.50
1921	2	9	2	0	1.000	14	10	10	2	4.00
1930	1	9	1	0	1.000	11	3	3	2	3.00
1933	1	9	1	0	1.000	12	5	3	0	5.00
Totals	163	1,220	92	44	.676	974	400	443	486	2.24

Babe Ruth's major league record — as a hitter

Year	Games played	At bat	Runs	Total hits
1914	5	10	1	2
1915	42	92	16	29
1916	67	136	18	37
1917	52	123	14	40
1918	95	317	50	95
1919	130	432	103	139
1920	142	458	158	172
1921	152	540	177	204
1922	110	403	94	128
1923	152	522	151	205
1924	153	529	143	200
1925	98	359	61	104
1926	152	495	139	184
1927	151	540	158	192
1928	154	536	163	173
1929	135	499	121	172
1930	145	518	150	186
1931	145	534	149	199
1932	133	457	120	156
1933	137	459	97	138
1934	125	365	78	105
1935	28	72	13	13
Totals	2,503	8,396	2,174	2,873

Two-base hits	Three-base hits	Home runs	Runs batted in	Batting average
1	0	0	0	.200
10	1	4	20	.315
5	3	3	16	.272
6	3	2	10	.325
26	11	11	64	.300
34	12	29	112	.322
36	9	54	137	.376
44	16	59	170	.378
24	8	35	96	.315
45	13	41	130	.393
39	7	46	121	.378
12	2	25	66	.290
30	5	47	155	.372
29	8	60	164	.356
29	8	54	142	.323
26	6	46	154	.345
28	9	49	153	.359
31	3	46	163	.373
13	5	41	137	.341
21	3	34	103	.301
17	4	22	84	.288
0	0	6	12	.181
506	136	714	2,209	.342

Henry "Hank" Aaron

Henry gave his bat a few practice swings and stepped into the batter's box. He twisted his right foot a couple of times to dig his spikes into the dirt. Then he looked out at the pitcher. Pitcher Al Downing of the Los Angeles Dodgers was looking into the catcher to get his sign. Then he nodded and went into his pitching motion. In came the pitch. It was an outside curve ball and Henry let it go by. Ball one.

Henry gripped his bat tighter and waited for the next pitch. Something inside told him to expect a fast ball and he set himself for it. In came the pitch. Henry swung hard and his bat made contact with the ball. Henry didn't wait to watch where the ball went. He was running as hard as he could toward first base. He knew he had hit the ball hard. But was it hit hard enough?

Henry was almost to first base when he heard the umpire shout, "Home run!"

Henry felt a great sense of relief. He slowed to a trot as he rounded first base. He could hear the crowd, over 53,000, on their feet yelling and shouting. Rockets began bursting overhead in the dark Atlanta sky. A huge number "715" flashed on and off the scoreboard.

He was rounding third, and he could see all his teammates swarming around home plate waiting for him to get there. His father was running over from the box seats. As he touched home plate it seemed that everybody was pounding him on the back. His father gave him a big hug. Then, as he went toward the stands, his mother came up to hug him too. She was screaming for joy and tears were running down her cheeks.

At 9:07 P.M. on April 8, 1974,

Henry Aaron had hit the 715th home run of his career, breaking Babe Ruth's record. He was the new home run king. "Thank God, it's over," Henry said. It seemed that he had been reaching for this moment for years. And for years the pressure had been increasing. Now it was over. He had done it. Already Henry could feel some of the knots in his stomach begin to loosen.

After the game, there was a big party in the Atlanta Braves' locker room. Champagne was opened and served in paper cups. TV cameras were in place. Newsmen from all over the world were there. "I'm glad it's all over," Henry told them. "Now I can settle down and have a real good season. The Braves can too, and that's what really counts."

The party lasted over an hour. Slowly the crowd began breaking up. Soon almost everybody was gone. Henry put his baseball glove and shoes into his locker. He looked around. The locker room was a mess. Empty paper cups were on the benches and lockers and all over the floor. At one end of the room, some TV crewmen were rolling up their lines and packing up their lights and cameras.

Henry sat down on a bench. "Well, that's over," he said to himself. The excitement of the day was gone, and he felt a little let down. "At last, I've broken Babe Ruth's record. And this looks like it's going to be a good year. But what then?" Somehow, retirement from baseball seemed near.

Henry had been playing major-league baseball for 20 years. He was 40 years old. Not old for a man, but old for a professional baseball player. After games now, he was often tired. Aches in his legs didn't go away in just a few hours as they used to. Playing baseball was becoming more work and less fun.

During spring training, Henry had worked very hard. He kept thinking to himself, "I've got to break Babe Ruth's record. I've got to break that record." And now he had done it. Without that goal to spur him on, would he ever be able to force himself to work that hard again?

Baseball hadn't always been work. Henry could remember when baseball had been nothing but fun. When he was young, he could play all day long and never feel really tired. It seemed that he was always throwing or catching or hitting a baseball.

When he was in grade school, Henry would meet his friends at the ball field. They didn't have regular teams. They didn't need any. If a lot of boys showed up, they chose sides. If there were only a few players, they played "move up." If only a couple, they played catch.

Henry even had a game he could

play all by himself at home. He had the street in front of his house marked off into boundaries. Using a broom handle and soda pop bottle caps, he would practice hitting. If he hit a bottle cap to the fire hydrant, he gave himself a single. Farther, to the neighbor's driveway, was a double. And if he hit one really well, it would go past the corner for a home run.

But Henry didn't get to play baseball or even his bottle cap game every time he pleased. There were chores to be done to help out around the house. Henry's father worked long hours at the shipyard down at the Mobile, Alabama, waterfront. He was a "rivet bucker." The furnace man on the job would throw red-hot rivets up to where he was working. Henry's father would catch them in a small metal bucket, then put them in the rivet holes and hold them with a tool against the back of the rivets while another man hammered the rivet heads flat. It was a hard, dangerous job. Henry's father made a steady living, but he didn't make much money.

There were eight children in the Aaron family. To help feed them all, the Aarons had a vegetable garden. One of Henry's chores was to keep it weeded. Sometimes, particularly when Henry wanted to play baseball, weeding the garden seemed like a waste of time. "Man," he'd tell himself, "working like this in the hot sun makes me tired. And the weeds grow three times faster than these dumb beans. Why can't we eat the weeds instead?"

Sometimes, after he had worked down a row of vegetables and out of sight of the house, he would crawl out the far end of the garden and run to join his friends at the ball field. Then, he would play baseball all day in the hot sun and hardly feel it.

When Henry was 11 years old, he helped his father build a new home for the family. The United States Army had torn down a supply depot that was no longer in use and there was lots of used lumber nearby. The whole family pitched in to help. Henry's job was pulling the nails out of the boards his father hauled to the new home site. Then he would straighten the nails he pulled out so that they could be used again. That way, they saved on new nails.

Other chores interfered with baseball too. Henry and his brother Herbert had to chop wood. Cooking at the Aarons' was done on a wood-burning stove and that called for a steady supply of cut wood if they were to eat.

Henry liked all sports. In high school, he played football, but baseball was his favorite. The high school didn't have a regular hardball team. During the summer, though, Henry got a chance to play regular hardball with the local Recreation Department League.

Henry played shortstop. Among the youngsters of the recreation league, he was a stand-out fielder and hitter. So when Henry heard that the Brooklyn Dodgers were going to hold a try-out camp in Mobile, he thought he should try out too. He was good, wasn't he? After all, Jackie Robinson played for the Dodgers. Maybe they'd give him a chance.

The camp was held at a field just outside of town. Henry rode his bike. As he pedaled along, he could see himself as a Dodger, hitting the game-winning home run. Or making a game-saving play at shortstop. By the time Henry got to the field, the future looked rosy.

For a while he watched batting practice and hung around the fence with other boys waiting their turn. Finally a coach came over to tell the boys what he wanted them to do. But he turned to Henry and said, "Young fella, you're too small to be a ballplayer. You better get on home."

Henry was stunned. All his dreams seemed smashed. He wanted to speak up, to tell the coach how wrong he was, but he couldn't. He was too shy. All he could do was bite his lip and turn away. Well, he'd try again next year.

Henry had better luck later on, though. A coach from the local semi-pro team, the Mobile Black Bears, saw him play one day and asked him to join their group. The Bears played on weekends because the members had to work on other jobs during the week. Quickly, Henry became their regular shortstop.

When Henry Aaron was 19 years old, he played for
the Jacksonville Tars. Veteran Manager Ben Geraghty
helped him to develop into an all-around player.

Henry can run fast when he has to. The first baseman has
just missed a wild throw from the infield. Henry is safe
on first.

Henry joined the Braves for spring training in 1954. Manager Charlie Grimm shakes his hand as he trots around third base after hitting a home run.

In 1956, Henry was one of the batting leaders in the National League, along with Wally Moon and Stan Musial.

Henry scores again. The run helped the Braves to win
a close game.

Henry runs after a long drive into left field. He caught the ball and made the put-out.

Home run number 715 — and Henry breaks Babe Ruth's record. He becomes the new home run king.

Henry's mother hugs him after he hit home run number
715. Another player holds the famous ball Henry hit.
It was a big day in Henry Aaron's baseball career.

He gained experience and at the end of the next season, when Henry was 17, he got another big break.

In the fall of 1951, the Indianapolis Clowns of the Negro American League came through Mobile on a tour. Their regular season had just ended and they were making a swing around to cities not on their regular schedule. They would play the local teams and earn some extra money. One Sunday, they played the Bears, and the Clowns' manager liked the way Henry fielded his position and swung his bat.

After the game, he asked Henry, "How would you like to play for the Clowns next year?"

"I sure would," Henry answered.

"Good. I'll mail you a contract next spring."

Henry was excited. He had been promised a contract to play for a real professional team. For months, Henry waited anxiously. Would the contract or spring ever come?

Finally, after what seemed like ages, both arrived. Henry boarded a train that would take him to Winston-Salem, North Carolina, where the Clowns were in spring training. Henry was 18 years old and just graduated from high school. He had never been away from home before. He was scared, but he was getting a chance to show how well he could play baseball, and that was the most important thing.

It was warm when Henry left Mobile, but during the long train ride through the mountains, the temperature dropped into the 40's. Henry didn't even have a jacket to keep him warm. He was still cold when he reached the spring training camp the next day. The chilly welcome the Clowns' players gave him did nothing to warm him, either. To them, Henry was just another kid they'd have to put up with until he was sent packing. Everybody ignored him.

On the field, it was no better. Henry hardly got a chance to take batting practice or do much fielding. Over a week went by and Henry was getting discouraged. The Clowns began playing other teams in spring training around North Carolina. But Henry still wasn't given a chance to play.

Then one afternoon, Henry saw his name on the line-up card. "At last." He took a deep breath. "I've got to do well," he said to himself. And he did — he hit two singles the first two times at bat and he made some good plays at shortstop.

Henry was happy with the way he had played, but the next day he was out of the line-up again. It seemed that no one took any notice. And for days, Henry sat on the bench. He couldn't understand it.

Then all of a sudden, Henry saw his name on the line-up card again. And again he was determined to do well. But would anyone take notice? That afternoon, Henry got four hits in four times at bat, and somebody did notice. Henry was made the regular shortstop when the season opened.

Henry continued to do well. Almost from the beginning of the regular season, he led the Negro American League in batting with a .467 average — nearly one hit in every two times at bat.

One of the ways the Clowns made money was to develop young players and then sell them to bigger and richer ball clubs. A teenage shortstop who could hit over .400 was certainly of interest. The Clowns' owner wrote to several ball clubs about him. One of them, the Braves, then of Milwaukee, Wisconsin, sent scout Dewey Griggs to look Henry over.

Griggs was used to traveling around to look at promising young ballplayers and wasn't expecting to see anything unusual. He went to the ball park and sat in the stands like any other fan. What he saw that day in Indianapolis, though, made him sit up. Henry got seven hits in eight times at bat, including two home runs and a bunt he beat out for a single.

Griggs was interested in Henry, but one thing made him pause. He noticed that Henry held his bat cross-handed. Normally a right-handed batter holds his bat with his right hand above his left hand. Henry was different. He held his left hand on top and his wrists crossed.

When the game was over, Griggs met Henry and asked him, "How is it that you bat cross-handed?"

"I don't know," Henry said. "I just started batting this way."

"Well," Griggs said, "it's harder to hit inside pitches that way and if you got hit on the wrist, you might be seriously hurt."

Henry said that he knew that, but had never bothered to change.

Griggs had his doubts. "If you ever play in the major leagues, the pitchers there will take advantage of that weakness. I'd advise you to change. Tomorrow, bat the normal way and let's see what happens."

The next day, Henry changed his hold on the bat and got three hits. Griggs was convinced. Henry had a very good batting eye and could really swing a bat. It didn't matter which way he held his bat, he could hit either way. And once he got used to holding it the normal way, he'd be better than ever. Griggs made an offer to the Clowns for Henry's contract. It was accepted, and Henry became a player in the Braves' organization.

First, the Braves sent Henry to their farm team in Eau Claire, Wisconsin, to finish out the season. In a short time, he was hitting at a .336 average, one hit in every three times at bat. He hit nine home runs, four triples, and 19 doubles and was voted Most Outstanding Rookie.

The next year, 1953, Henry was sent to a tougher league, the South Atlantic League, to play for the Tars of Jacksonville, Florida.

Ben Geraghty, the manager, told Henry this was going to be a tougher league for more than one reason. "There has never been a black player in this league before. You and your teammates Horace Garner and Felix Mantilla will be the first. Jackie Robinson broke the color line in the major leagues. You'll be doing it here. But this is the South, so things could get rough."

Henry nodded. "I understand. I'm

here to help the team, not to hurt it."

Geraghty was pleased. "That's the spirit. Our fans want a good baseball team too. Play good ball, and they'll be cheering for you."

At first, things were very rough. Henry, Horace, and Felix were booed and called ugly names. It was bad at home in Jacksonville. It was worse when they visited other cities in the league. Geraghty did his best to cheer his players up and to help them over the rougher spots. And gradually, Henry began to notice a change, at least at home. There were fewer boos and even some cheers from the fans.

As the season went on, the cheering became louder. The Jacksonville Tars were in first place. It looked as if they would win their first pennant in 48 years. Late in the season Jacksonville did clinch the pennant, and Henry was moved to the outfield to gain experience.

Henry won the batting crown with a .362 average and was elected the league's Most Valuable Player. It was quite a season.

When spring training came around the next year, Henry was invited to take part in the Braves' major-league camp. The Braves' manager wanted to look him over, but it seemed that the team already had all the players they needed. Henry was glad to practice with the Braves' top players even if it wasn't going to be permanent.

Then an accident happened. One of the Braves' outfielders broke his ankle sliding into third base. For the practice game the next day, Henry started in left field. It was a good chance, and Henry didn't waste it. He got three hits, including a long, line drive home run.

"I think you're my new left fielder," the Braves' manager said.

Henry was 20 years old and had been

in professional baseball just two years. And now he was the starting left fielder for a major-league team. He had done well in the minor leagues and he had done well in spring training. But could he continue to make good through a regular season?

The opening game was in Cincinnati. Henry was nervous. He was so anxious to do well. The pressure was on him, and in five times at bat he went without a hit.

Then the Braves moved back to their home park for a series with St. Louis. The pressure built up again, but this time Henry connected with the ball for a double his first time up to bat. It was his first major-league hit. Henry felt a great relief. He had broken the ice.

A week later, the Braves were on the road again for a return match with the St. Louis Cardinals, this time in St. Louis. It was still early April and the weather had been uncertain — first rain, then shine. Only a few thousand people came out to the ball park that day. The stadium looked almost empty.

In the second inning, the fans saw a young ballplayer named Henry Aaron come to bat. Henry let two balls go past, then swung at a fast ball, waist high. He connected and the ball soared out to deep left center field. It cleared the fence for a home run, Henry Aaron's first major-league home run.

As Henry rounded the bases, hardly a cheer was heard. There were just a few thousand people in the stadium that day. Could any of them have guessed that 20 years later Henry Aaron would hit his 715th home run before a crowd of 53,000 and a TV audience of millions?

Not even Henry Aaron could know that.

Henry Aaron's hitting record in professional baseball, 1954-1975

Year	Games played	At bat	Runs	Total hits
1954	122	468	58	131
1955	153	602	105	189
1956	153	609	106	200
1957	151	615	118	198
1958	153	601	109	196
1959	154	629	116	223
1960	153	590	102	172
1961	155	603	115	197
1962	156	592	127	191
1963	161	631	121	201
1964	145	570	103	187
1965	150	570	109	181
1966	158	603	117	168
1967	155	600	113	184
1968	160	606	84	174
1969	147	547	100	164
1970	150	516	103	154
1971	139	495	95	162
1972	129	449	75	119
1973	120	392	84	118
1974	112	340	47	91
1975	137	465	45	109
Totals	3,213	12,093	2,152	3,708

Two-base hits	Three-base hits	Home runs	Runs batted in	Batting average
27	6	13	69	.280
37	9	27	106	.314
34	14	26	92	.328
27	6	44	132	.322
34	4	30	95	.326
46	7	39	123	.355
20	11	40	126	.292
39	10	34	120	.327
28	6	45	128	.323
29	4	44	130	.319
30	2	24	95	.328
40	1	32	89	.318
23	1	44	127	.279
37	3	39	109	.307
33	4	29	86	.287
30	3	44	97	.300
26	1	38	118	.298
22	3	47	118	.327
10	0	34	77	.265
12	1	40	96	.301
16	0	20	69	.268
16	2	12	60	.234
616	98	745	2,262	.307

SCHOLASTIC BIOGRAPHY

☐ MP44075-6	Bo Jackson: Playing the Games	$2.95
☐ MP41836-X	Custer and Crazy Horse: A Story of Two Warriors	$2.75
☐ MP44570-7	The Death of Lincoln: A Picture History of the Assassination	$2.95
☐ MP43866-2	The Defenders	$2.75
☐ MP43210-9	Faithful Friend: The Story of Florence Nightingale	$2.75
☐ MP44767-X	The First Woman Doctor	$2.95
☐ MP42218-9	Frederick Douglass Fights for Freedom	$2.50
☐ MP43628-7	Freedom Train: The Story of Harriet Tubman	$2.75
☐ MP43730-5	George Washington: The Man Who Would Not Be King	$2.75
☐ MP43800-X	Great Escapes of World War II	$2.75
☐ MP42402-5	Harry Houdini: Master of Magic	$2.75
☐ MP42404-1	Helen Keller	$2.50
☐ MP44230-9	I Have a Dream: The Story of Martin Luther King	$2.50
☐ MP42395-9	Jesse Jackson: A Biography	$2.75
☐ MP43503-5	Jim Abbott: Against All Odds	$2.75
☐ MP41344-9	John Fitzgerald Kennedy: America's 35th President	$2.50
☐ MP41159-4	Lost Star: The Story of Amelia Earhart	$2.75
☐ MP42659-1	Mr. President: A Book of U.S. Presidents	$2.75
☐ MP42644-3	Our 41st President George Bush	$2.50
☐ MP43481-0	Pocahontas and the Strangers	$2.75
☐ MP41877-7	Ready, Aim, Fire! The Real Adventures of Annie Oakley	$2.75
☐ MP41183-7	Secret Missions: Four True-Life Stories	$2.50
☐ MP43052-1	The Secret Soldier: The Story of Deborah Sampson	$2.50
☐ MP43605-8	Sole Survivor	$2.95
☐ MP44055-1	Squanto, Friend of the Pilgrims	$2.75
☐ MP42560-9	Stealing Home: The Story of Jackie Robinson	$2.75
☐ MP44353-4	The Story of My Life	$2.75
☐ MP42403-3	The Story of Thomas Alva Edison, Inventor: The Wizard of Menlo Park	$2.50
☐ MP44431-X	They Led the Way: 14 American Women	$2.95
☐ MP42904-3	The Wright Brothers at Kitty Hawk	$2.75

Available wherever you buy books, or use this order form.

Scholastic Inc., P.O. Box 7502, 2931 East McCarty Street, Jefferson City, MO 65102

Please send me the books I have checked above. I am enclosing $_____ (please add $2.00 to cover shipping and handling). Send check or money order — no cash or C.O.D.s please.

Name _____

Address _____

City _____ State/Zip _____

Please allow four to six weeks for delivery. Available in the U.S. only. Sorry, mail orders are not available to residents of Canada. Prices subject to change. BIO1190